I0556515

NIGHTS TO REMEMBER

Feeding My Addictions
Kinks, Chains, and Everything

Short Stories
Volume I

Khali'a Ishana

Nights to Remember by Khali'a Ishana

Published by The Champagne Connection
P O BOX 87468 – Chicago IL 60680

This is a work of fiction. Names, characters, places, and incidents either are the products of the author's imagination or are used fictitiously. Any resemblance to actual persons, living or dead, businesses, companies, events, or locales is entirely coincidental.

Cover by harbingerdesign of Fiverr
Library of Congress Registration Number on File
ISBN: 978-0-9749387-4-5
Printed in the United States

LEGAL NOTICES AND/OR DISCLAIMERS:

The material supplied here reflects the author's opinion as of the publishing date. The author retains the right to revise and update her view in light of the new circumstances due to the rapid rate at which things change. The book is just meant to provide information. Although every effort has been taken to ensure the accuracy of the material in this book, neither the author nor her affiliates/partners accept any liability for any mistakes, inaccuracies, or omissions. Any slights towards individuals or groups are inadvertent. If legal or related advice is required, a fully certified professional's services should be sought out. This book is not meant to be a source of accounting or legal advice. You should be informed of any regulations in your nation and state that regulate business dealings or other commercial activities. Any mention of a living or deceased person or company is completely accidental.

TABLE OF CONTENTS

LAP DANCING

As Gabrielle dressed, she knew tonight would be special. Uncertain as to how the night would unfold, she wanted to make certain she was prepared for everything. Normally, she was never fond of underwear; however, tonight was different. Her body longed for pleasure, and her pussy ached for relief. She carefully slipped into the sexiest pair of thongs hoping they would provide the friction her clitoris needed. Because her breasts were as near perfect as possible, she opted only for a sheer lacy blouse followed by a matching mini-shirt. In case of emergency, easy access was assured.

She arrived in her limo at a nude bar she had seen advertised in an obscure newspaper and sat at a table near the stage. Tonight, she did not want to miss anything.

By the third dancer, Gabrielle's nipples were so hard she needed relief. Without thinking, she placed her hand in her blouse and began caressing her breast. The dancer noticed and started gyrating her hips toward Gabrielle. It seemed as though she was stripping solely for Gabrielle. As the dancer slid her fingers in and out of her own pussy, Gabrielle mimicked the actions. She lifted her skirt and rubbed her clit with her middle finger while her left hand continued to caress her nipples. Gabrielle's pussy got wetter and wetter, but she craved more. She nodded to the dancer, and it was not too long before the dancer was standing at Gabrielle's table. To entice her to continue, Gabrielle slid two large bills on the table. The dancer moved closer and closer

1

and continued to play with her own body, rotating between her nipples and her pussy. Gabrielle was turned on by large breasts, and the dancer had the best set she had ever seen. Gabrielle removed her hand from her own body and began to touch the dancer's body, focusing on her breast, her big, beautiful breast. The dancer moved closer until her nipples were in Gabrielle's mouth. Gabrielle's clitoris was so hard she thought it would explode. As she sucked, the dancer moaned. Not wanting this moment to end, Gabrielle put her finger inside the dancer's wet, bushy mound and was turned on even more. She removed her fingers, and the dancer licked them dry, one by one. The dancer knelt in front of Gabrielle, lifted her skirt to her waist, and slowly licked Gabrielle's pussy. As she continued, Gabrielle relaxed more and more until her body trembled with pleasure and relief. But the dancer continued licking, sucking, and chewing. Gabrielle came over and over again. Once the dancer felt Gabrielle was completely satisfied, she stopped. She kissed Gabrielle's lips and left.

Gabrielle was dancing alone when another dancer, Jade, came up to her and started grinding her ass right up on Gabrielle's front. Gabrielle instinctively put her hands on Jade's hips. Jade was grinding hard on Gabrielle as she bent over, revealing the top of her thong from the back of her pants. Gabrielle was getting hotter by the minute. Jade stood up straight and leaned back on Gabrielle's chest and dropped her head backward onto Gabrielle's shoulder. Gabrielle, feeling frisky, playfully bit Jade's neck. Jade, also started feeling really good by now, turned right into Gabrielle's lips and kissed her. Gabrielle was a little taken aback by this, but then she quickly got over it. Who cares, she thought, it is my night out, and I am going to have fun! She returned the kiss.

The girls soon turned, facing each other, dancing up on each other, sharing kisses here and there along the way. Gabrielle would lean up next to Jade and say, "You are so fucking hot girl, the things I'd love to do to you!" Jade would just smile, almost like saying the feelings were mutual. Hands would slip to the others' sweaty breasts here and there for a quick tease. The floor was packed, and the place was hot.

2

The girls decided to slide back to their table in the corner, which happened to be extremely dark. The dance floor is where all the lights were, so the tables were not really paid much attention to at this point.

The girls slipped back to the table together, where they sat on the same side, drinking their new cold drinks. Jade leaned over to Gabrielle's ear and softly whispered, "Well, show me what that mouth has been asking for all night." The girls embraced in a steamy kiss. Gabrielle was so horny from the teasing that Jade's body had been giving her all night. She could barely control herself. She grabbed Jade's hair in her fist and pulled her neck to the side, letting Jade first feel her breath on her neck, and then she gently bit her again. She would kiss and bite Jade and then run her tongue up Jade's neck to her ear. She would nibble Jade's ear lobe as Jade was still accepting everything Gabrielle was giving her.

Gabrielle had her right hand holding back Jade's hair while her left hand traveled down Jade's neck to her chest. She grabbed Jade's nearly exposed breast tightly. Jade threw her head back again, trying to catch her breath. She was breathing heavily from the dancing and couldn't catch her breath now that she was being seduced by Gabrielle. Gabrielle had her fill of Jade's chest and wanted to feel Jade's pussy on her fingers. Jade directed Gabrielle's eyes to her and mouthed, "I'm not wearing any panties!" with a devilish grin. Gabrielle slid her hand down Jade's stomach and down the top on her thigh. She reached her knee and slid her hand to the inside of Jade's thigh, then slowly slid her hand up Jade's leg under her skirt. Jade opened her legs a little to invite Gabrielle's hand in further. Jade pulled her skirt up with a clenched fist around the bottom of her skirt. She needed something to grab and hard. She was ready to come unglued any second.

Gabrielle played with Jade's wet pussy lips, teasing the opening of her pussy with each swift motion of her fingers near the opening but then going around it. Jade thrust her hips forward slightly as Gabrielle would get so close but never go in. Gabrielle was still massaging Jade's ears and neck with her tongue and occasionally Jade's lips as she'd turn to Gabrielle's lips with her own. Gabrielle slid and waited until it seemed Jade could no longer take the torture of those fingers skipping over her pussy, and Gabrielle slid them in, deep. Jade moaned loud enough that Gabrielle heard her over the music and felt the vibration on her lips, which were on Jade's neck at the time. Jade wanted her so badly. She wanted Gabrielle to fuck her right here, right now. Gabrielle could tell.

Gabrielle slipped under the table, unnoticed by the rest of the bar crowd. She was still gliding her fingers in and out of Jade's wet pussy. Jade was enjoying every minute of it. Gabrielle slid Jade's legs wider. Jade loved not being able to see what Gabrielle was doing. It was such a welcomed surprise when she would change up what she was doing, and Jade didn't know ahead of time. Gabrielle pulled her fingers from Jade's pussy and licked them clean. She grabbed Jade's legs with both her hands, squeezed gently, and shoved her face into Jade's waiting pussy. Jade couldn't hold back her moans.

Thank goodness the music was so loud, and the corner was dark, or they'd have an audience for sure. Gabrielle had her face so far into Jade's pussy that she'd have to stop to breathe every once in a while just before ramming her face back into Jade's pussy. In the seconds it took her to breathe, she slid her fingers back into Jade's sweet hole. Jade was getting fucked just as she'd begged for just a few minutes earlier. Gabrielle tended to every need of Jade's pussy. She'd fucked her as hard and deep as she could with her tongue and then slid her tongue out and up Jade's lips, separating them just enough to reach Jade's clit. She'd flick her tongue all over Jade's clit. Then she'd latch onto her clit and suck hard and thrust her fingers into Jade's pussy. Jade was getting closer and closer to cumming with every thrust of Gabrielle's fingers. Gabrielle released Jade's clit stuck her tongue out, and shook her head violently from side to side, catching jade's clit with every pass. Gabrielle would then put her wide tongue out as far as she could and lick Jade's wet pussy from the back to the front.

She'd repeat these patterns again and again. Jade couldn't stand it anymore; she was ready to cum. It was like an eruption inside of her that was building up, and she could not wait to explode. She screamed at the top of her lungs as Gabrielle sucked her clit hard inside her mouth and fucked her hard and fast with her fingers. Gabrielle could feel Jade's pussy contract around her fingers. She didn't want to stop until Jade was satisfied. She sucked harder and harder still as Jade was thrusting forward with pleasure. Gabrielle fucked harder and harder through Jade's immense orgasm.

Gabrielle's hands were now full of Jade's juice, and her mouth was trying to capture every drop. Jade tasted amazing on her lips. She had relaxed her body to the back of her chair as Gabrielle pulled her hand out of Jade's content pussy. Gabrielle licked through every crease of Jade's pussy, and then she cleaned her hand with her own tongue. She kissed Jade's clit one last time before returning to her seat next to Jade.

Jade was sitting there recovering from her intense orgasm, smiling, waiting for Gabrielle. She grabbed Gabrielle and kissed her, licking any juices that Gabrielle may have missed on her face and lips. "You are fucking amazing!" she insisted to Gabrielle.

Gabrielle quickly straightened her clothing and returned to the limo. She knew tonight would be special, a night to remember, and special it was.

THE WORKS

As she approached the door, she hoped she would not be disappointed. Club LaRambla was an anything-goes club, and Nadia had grand expectations. She wanted to look as sexy as she could, so she wore her hair down. She took exceptional care when applying her makeup. Her eyes and lips have been her most striking features, and tonight she did her best to accentuate them. As she entered Club LaRambla, she was escorted to a table and given a menu. When she opened the menu, she found exactly what she wanted—***cum on a disc***. After making her selection, she was prompted to choose "the ingredients." She chooses eight of the best-looking men and four of the sexiest women she had ever laid eyes on. She placed her order with a scantily clad waiter and sipped a glass of champagne as she waited for her fantasy to be prepared.

In the next 15 minutes, Nadia was blindfolded by her waiter and taken to a chair in the middle of the next room. While she waited, she realized she was being undressed by someone with the softest hands. Her clothes fell to the floor. She felt several lips kissing her body, nibbling her nipples, and sucking the lips of her pussy. As her body began to respond, the petting stopped, and she was led to a round disc and placed on her back. Her hair was arranged, and her legs gently spread. The blindfold was removed, so Nadia could see the women who would make love to her and the men who would be instrumental in fulfilling her fantasy.

Each man stood at least 6 feet tall with an average dick size of 10" in length. The women gently applied restraints to Nadia's arms and legs. Her husband entered the room, sounded the gong, and ordered the men to fuck, suck and cover his wife with cum. She had not expected Chandra to attend, but she had to admit that his presence heightened her pleasure. Nadia enjoyed two things—fulfilling her sexual needs and being her husband's sex slave. Her husband sat on a loveseat and watched as each man bent over Nadia and thrust his dick in her mouth. At times Nadia was ordered to suck as many as three men simultaneously. Chandra watched as the women devoured Nadia's pussy like a pack of hungry wolves after a major kill. He loved seeing his wife driven wild with sexual ecstasy. He loved it when she became so excited that she would moan for more and beg for it to stop at the same time.

By now, one of the men, Jon, could not wait to get into action, and she had to tell him to slow down and be gentle. Then he wanted to linger when he got to her shaved cunt, but after a few licks, she hurried him on to the next stage.

Her nipples were quite long and quite hard. He first licked them, cupping her tits with his hands, then started sucking hard, then dropped his hand down and searched with his finger until he found the entrance to her vajayjay. It felt wonderfully wet and warm; he moved his finger gently around, withdrew it, stroked it along the entire length of her crack, and then slipped it back in again.

She loved every moment and was making noises as if she'd never had it this good. Jon's dick was rubbing up against the inside of her thigh as he worked his middle-aged magic; she arched her back and angled it so that the head of it touched the lips of her cunt. He then took his dick in hand and rubbed it up and down her slit. She began to gasp for breath, and it didn't take long before her body started to shake quite violently, "Holy fuck, I'm cumming," she screamed, digging her long nails into his shoulders until they fetched blood.

Another man, Devyn, settled down in short order and slid beneath him so she could take his throbbing cock into her mouth. He let out a yell as she absorbed most of it, and then she grabbed onto his balls, pulling, and squeezing them. It was a little painful, but with her soft lips sliding slowly up and down his shaft, it did not seem to matter. Jon was dying to cum and prayed she'd let him come in her mouth; nobody had ever let him do that before.

Tightening her grip around the base of his dick, she quickened the pace until he could feel his hot sperm racing upwards, and although he gallantly warned her when he was about to ejaculate, she soldiered on and swallowed the lot. Even after pulling his dick out of her mouth, she kept licking the dripping end, making sure all the while it was captured on camera.

Jon was breathing heavily and starting to perspire, but Nadia was not about to let him slack off.

"Lick me out and lick me out good," she commanded, spreading her legs to give him easy access. With his face between her thighs, he separated the lips of her tight pussy with his fingers and then began to give her a thorough tongue lashing.

Jon had always prided himself on his eating-out ability, and he sailed his king-sized tongue up and down her crack until she cried out, "Oh my God, oh my God," and then seemed to lose her mind as she had the biggest fucking orgasm she'd ever had.

Even though her body hadn't finished shaking, she yelled for him to shove it in and fuck her. Jon knelt on the bed, drew her quivering pussy towards him, and rammed it in up to the hilt.

She was gulping for air and flailing her arms as he pulled on her thighs and impaled her. Sparks seemed to course throughout his body as he pounded her pussy. Her tits were bouncing in every direction, and she was biting hard on her lip as he made the last final thrusts. There seemed to be no end to his semen; as it kept flowing and flowing, she gripped harder onto his ass, pulling him further and further into her.

Nadia winced as a woman, Moira, swung a cane forcefully against her naked backside for the sixth time. The jolt of pain nearly caused her to gag on another man, Harry's cock, as it was pushed into the beginning of her throat. Nadia felt the all too familiar rush of pleasure as her tongue moved frantically on his penis and pain as Moira wielded the cane against her naked flesh. Her juices were running down her inner thigh in a virtual torrent. No matter how many times they acted out this scene, her arousal never diminished. Nadia guessed that she would soon be filled by Harry's thick cock, and she prayed that Moira would let her lick her pussy as he was impaling her.

Nadia felt Harry pull his prick from her mouth, and his strong hands spun her around onto her back, and within seconds she felt him thrust into her until his balls slapped against her arise. His manhood had met little resistance as she was dripping after Moira's flogging while having Harry in her mouth. She loved to suck his cock as much as he loved her doing it.

Her eyes were shut, and the cool sheets brought welcoming relief to her burning buttocks. She felt Moira lower herself onto her face, and Nadia reached out her tongue to find the woman's dripping slit. Her tongue gathered up Moira's juices from her labia as she ran it from bottom to top before nibbling at the erect clitoris at its apex. The taste was familiar and the reaction predictable, but it still brought Nadia joy when she knew that she had given Moira the release she sought.

Harry was moving in and out of her frantically now, and Nadia knew he was close. "Where would he cum?" she wondered to herself. She hoped he would come inside her and spray the walls of her cervix with his cum. Lately, he had taken a liking to pulling out and spraying her tummy and breasts with warm cum. She was in a dreamy state as she contemplated Harry's options. He might fill her mouth or maybe Moira's. Whichever method he chose, Nadia knew that she would cum loudly as he came; she always did.

Nadia felt Moira push her clit hard down onto Nadia's tongue. A sign of her impending climax. Nadia renewed her efforts with vigor and was rewarded by a squealing from the woman sitting on her face and a flood of liquid entering her mouth and nose and covering her face. Moira moved forward, and Nadia felt Harry's stiffness leave the wet warmth of her pussy, and she heard the unmistakable sound of

Moira accepting and then swallowing her husband's seed as he screamed his release to the ceiling with a loud "Yeeeeeeeeees!"

Her heightened state of arousal and the sounds of her two best friends achieving their climax caused Nadia to experience an intense one of her own. As Moira removed herself from her face, Nadia let out a long, loud "Aaaaaargh!" and bucked around on the bed for several seconds before laying back and gasping air deep into her lungs.

Before she had recovered, Harry covered her mouth with his, and his tongue probed inside as he kissed her passionately. As he pulled away Moira's mouth, and tongue replaced his and Nadia could taste the distinctive flavor of her husband's semen on the older woman's tongue.

Nadia was in a wonderful, exhausted state as she lay down there, but she was dragged from her post-coital bliss.

Nadia laughed as she replied, "Always Moira. What about your old lady slit? Not dried up yet?"

Nadia flinched as Moira landed a loud smack on her already punished buttocks in answer to her cheekiness. "I can keep up with your young ones just fine Missy," she playfully scolded Nadia before saying evilly, "I just hope there is one amongst them that wants to tan your hide EVERY bloody night, just for your rudeness. If there isn't, I will be doing it myself, you sing my words, young lady!"

Nadia had sucked all the men and had been expertly fucked by all the men. The women sucked Nadia's pussy one last time because they enjoyed the taste of Nadia's juices mixed with the cum of the others. The men were so turned on by this that each had an erection that could not be ignored. The women sucked their dicks, but this offered no relief. Nadia ordered the men to cum on her. With this, Nadia knew she would finally be satisfied. Still encircling Nadia, each man stroked his hardened member until they came. Nadia felt the cum land on her body. With each drop, her body convulsed with uncontrollable orgasms. She was filled with cum from head to toe. As she lay limp with pleasure, out of the corner of her eye, she glimpsed Chandra as he relieved his load deep in the ass of one of the women who helped to give Nadia a night to remember.

THE DELECTABLE DELI

Carmen often fantasized about having another man in bed with her and her husband. She often wanted a man who would enjoy fucking her, sucking her husband's dick, and enjoy being fucked by her husband. Then they met Sean. By all indicators, he fit the bill. Both Carmen and her husband found him attractive. Sean had verbally stated he would love to have sex with both of them, and he was a committed bi-sexual. Sean would be visiting Carmen and Peter tonight, and they decided that tonight was the night.

When Sean arrived, Carmen noticed he was more open and seemed more adventurous than usual. When he greeted her with a hug, he let his hand caress her butt. He had never done that before, and this aroused Carmen to no end. She later whispered to Peter that tonight was the night, and she left the room momentarily before dessert. She slipped into the lingerie Peter bought for this occasion and rejoined the men at the table. After dessert, she poured the wine, turned on the music, and asked both of them to join her on the patio near the pool. As they sat, she stood and began dancing and stripping to the soft sounds of Fore Play. She allowed the subtle drumbeat from the music to penetrate her consciousness and moved her hips, discarded her clothing, and fingered her pussy until it was dripping wet. She then put her fingers in Sean's and Peter's mouths for them to lick clean. It would not be long before she had a dick in her pussy and one in her ass. But she did not want to rush it. She wanted this night to last as long as possible, to be a night to remember.

She turned toward Sean, whose dick was rock hard, and started to undress him. With his help, this was accomplished quickly. Now to Peter, who had started to undress as he watched his wife strip. Soon they were all naked, and Carmen fell to her knees and began sucking Sean's dick. Peter was curious and excited about this experience with Sean.

Peter decided he was ready, so he reached for Sean's cock.

Peter thought to himself, "Sean's cock wasn't as big as I had imagined it to be. It appeared to be rubbery and wrinkled in Carmen's hand." Peter noticed that when Carmen stretched it, it was obvious that the four inches she was fondling would probably double when erect. He was excited about this.

PETER:

Sean's balls were meaty and hung low. My hand went to the young man's balls, and while he might not have even expected me to do it, he did not protest.

I kneaded his balls while Carmen bent down and took Sean's cock in her mouth, and the young man groaned, leaning his head back and looking up at the ceiling as my wife went down on him.

Sean's nerves evaporated as his cock grew, and it was not more than a minute later that his cock was hard. His beige manhood was long and tapered, thick at the base and tapering down to the head. "Now this is just what I want," thought Peter.

A little more than half of the 8" was slick with my wife's saliva, and when I offered to see whether I could get it wetter, Carmen handed me Sean's prong before climbing up onto the couch while undoing her bikini bottom.

Straddling Sean, she pushed her lightly furred pussy into Sean's face while I watched from behind. From the sounds coming out of both of them, it was clear that the young man was lapping Carmen's cunt, and she was loving it.

As Sean's hands came up and squeezed my wife's plump bottom, I bowed my head down and let my lips slide down Sean's tool, my tongue working as I did.

"Big boy," I thought to myself as my mouth strained to accommodate the girth of the bottom part of the shaft. He was going to stretch out Carmen's pussy nicely with this hunk of meat because I could only get down an inch or so farther than my wife had and was forced to use my hand on the base of his manhood.

I heard Sean mutter that he was going to cum, so I stopped for a minute, taking his member out of my mouth and cradling the throbbing cock gently. A bead of pre-cum formed on the tip, but Sean had managed to keep from cumming, so I just jacked him off while he dug his fingers into Carmen's rear.

"You got him ready, Babe?" Carmen asked, and when she saw the gleaming spear was pointing right at her, she giggled and lowered herself down onto him while I positioned him to impale her properly.

"Ooh!" Carmen moaned as her pussy enveloped Sean's cook, and she let out a louder groan when he fully penetrated her with his entire cock.

"She likes big cocks," I told Sean from over Carmen's shoulder, and while that was true, she likes cocks of all shapes and sizes, even mine.

Carmen was gyrating on Sean's lap, running her hands through her short blonde hair while enjoying the ride. I squeezed her small titties as I knelt beside the two of them, leaning over and running my tongue under Carmen's arm, licking her buttery smooth armpit and making her squeal like she always did.

I crawled down off the couch and lowered my swim trunks. My cock was dripping as I gently stroked it while watching Sean fuck my wife, the sight of that thick stump stretching Carmen's pussy was making me fight to keep from cumming.

Sean and Carmen changed their positions and joined me on the floor, with my wife on her back and our former paperboy mounting her missionary style. Sean seemed startled to see me naked and stroking my modest member but didn't miss a stroke, and when Carmen begged him to go harder, he accommodated her. The slapping sounds of their sweaty bodies as they slammed together was music to my ears, and when I was afraid I could hold back no longer, Carmen came for the second time.

My fingers ran over the soft curves of her hips and thighs as he explored the wet lips and slid into her. My left hand reached past to rub her clit as my right hand grabbed at her ass, and my mouth nibbled her inner thigh. His hand withdrew, and from between her legs, I saw both of his hands grabbing her breasts firmly, kneading the flesh.

My mouth now set upon her pussy with intensity. I consumed her clit and gently sucked it in while my tongue flicked and teased it harder. I alternated that with tasting her sweetness inside, digging my tongue deep inside her pussy, fucking it with firm wet motions, then licking the inner and outer lips. Like a blind man memorizing every inch of her with my mouth.

I changed pressures and techniques regularly, ensuring every millimeter of her skin had been given attention and explored. Between that and the new man's hands groping her large breasts and sucking her nipples, her body was inching quickly to orgasm anyway. As she frantically ran her fingers through my hair, I guided her hand to his waist.

With no further provocation needed, she unbuckled his pants. I felt his side of the blanket go up as he removed his pants, freeing his hard cock to her caress. She explored his dick and balls with a tentative touch. Experienced but having held any but mine for 10 years. Familiar motions but foreign, too, as she stroked his dick. The weight, shape, and feel telling her this wasn't her husband's cock. The heat in his skin betrayed his desire. The soft skin contrasted the hardness below. His head was firm and leaking already. I continued licking her as she explored him.

Her fingers ran through his precum and spread it along his length. The naughtiness of the moment added to the sensations of my tongue and his fingers on her nipples until she exploded. Her orgasm convulsed as my licking intensified, and his hands guided her to new heights. Her pussy squeezing and contracting over and over again. Waves of bliss curled her toes and excited her nipples until our touches were too much. She pried him off her breasts, and her pushing on my head told me to stop licking.

You could hear her heavy breathing in a moment of calm before she pushed him over, got on all fours, and began licking his shaft. I moved to the side and watched the moment. As my wife let a new cock slide into her mouth. Sliding up and down the shaft, her hands stroking him harder and sometimes straying gently over his testicles. I love that feeling, and apparently, so did he by the loud moaning she already had him doing. She patted the bed next to him and slipped my pants off, and I joined them. Side by side, she alternated whose cock she sucked. Each either enjoyed her warm mouth's attention or the show she gave while she sucked the other one. He slid off the bed and moved behind her.

He grabbed her hips, and she guided his cock inside. I was expecting her to press the condom issue, but she was either unaware or, more likely, beyond caring. He didn't make love; he didn't have tentative first-time sex like this was a date gone very right. No, he fucked her. Hard and deep. Making every stroke count. His hips slapping against her ass. She struggled to keep my dick in her mouth. She slid over and rolled onto her side, his hips moving behind her and giving me a perfect view of my wife getting laid in front of me. His cock was wet as it slid in and out of her pink pussy. Her smooth, shaved lips sliding up and down his shaft.

After a moment of searing this memory into my head, knowing I will be jerking off to this forever, I moved my attention back to her breasts. I kissed them all over, and using my tongue made each nipple hard. Then I grabbed and squeezed them. My passion overriding sense and gentleness. She called my name, and I knew she was close again. I spoke to her encouraging her to fuck him. Telling her what a hot little fuck toy she was.

He took the hint and added in how great he felt. How he was going to drain his balls in her. I told her fuck him. Fuck Sean's cock hard.

Cum on it. She looked so hot that I ran my cock along her breasts and back into her mouth. She took it in, and I slid a few inches back and forth. Fucked at both ends she came again. Sucking hard on my cock as her pussy squeezed down on his cock.

It was too much for Sean, who also came. Erupting into her pussy and draining himself in her womb. She felt his hot cum adding to hers inside and warming them both. As he pulled out, she shook with pleasure. I wasted no time and slid into her still-spasming slit. Using the tip of my cock I shoved all his cum back into her. Then slid fully inside. Her pussy was warm and swollen against me. The excitement of the moment caused me to leak instantly into her. I saw Sean slide up and slip his still semi-hard cock into her mouth. She looked right into my eyes as she sucked him in and firmly began working him again.

I pinned both her hands by her waist. Sean and I were using her, and she was willingly giving herself to us. He came in her mouth faster than I thought was possible, and she stared at me while she swallowed. I was climbing quickly past the point of no return myself, and that sent me over.

Soon I erupted, telling her that was the hottest fucking thing I had ever seen. Barely coherent phrases were spilling out. She was my hot wife. Fucking loved her. Fuck yes, suck his cock. Each sentence true and punctuated by my dick shooting more cum into her. With a final push, I sent every drop as deep into her as I could. Spent, I pulled out and let her relax. Her red pussy lips were swollen and leaking more cum than I had ever seen in her.

"Gonna cum," Sean grunted. "What should..."

"Cum in her pussy," I said, trying to answer the question fast enough. "Plant your seed deep in her cunt."

The lean and athletic young man arched his body, and as he let out a series of grunts that were probably timed to his ejaculations, Carmen sighed with pleasure.

"So good," Carmen whispered to Sean. "Let my husband in for a second.

As Sean climbed off my wife, I assumed the position, her ravaged pussy wide open, and as I slid into the gooey cauldron, I managed to hold off for a bit, long enough to enjoy Sean dropping his spent dick into Carmen's mouth before I erupted, sending what felt like a massive load of my own into the mix.

"You guys are crazy," Sean gasped while Carmen sucked on his dick, and I climbed off of my wife. "I thought you two were-you know-normal people. Like my folks."

"We are," I said, and Carmen choked a little at the mention of Sean's parents, who had been' guests' of ours several times over the years. "Just normal horny folks."

Sean's eyes were bugging out when he saw me go back down between Carmen's parted thighs and enter her again, only this time with my tongue instead of my dick, but with his dick in Carmen's mouth, he had other things to think about, as did I.

What a night to remember.

SEKA

Seka owned a condo on the penthouse level of one of the most magnificent oceanfront high-rise buildings with views of both the ocean and the mountains. The view on any given day was absolutely breathtaking. Because she used this condo as a private getaway, she felt free and more relaxed whenever she stayed here. An early riser, she cherished the sunrises and enjoyed being greeted by the sun.

When she watched the sunrise from the beach, she imagined her nude body being massaged and warmed and her nipples being caressed by the sun's rays. As she lay on the beach, she could feel the sun flirting with her crotch, lightly caressing her pussy. She became aware of a gentle arousal slowly engulfing her body and causing her clitoris to swell. Unable to resist the overwhelming ecstasy building in her body, her pussy just kept getting wetter and wetter. As the sun continued to rise, Seka gently massaged her clitoris with her right hand, using two of her fingers.

Seka stretched her lithe body to its limits, moaning aloud at the same time. The chocolate-hued beauty was nude, with the exception of a black bandana wrapped around her forehead and a golden anklet leaving the rest of her body bared for the sun's caress. The sun was still high in the sky, licking at her dark skin, glistening with a thin layer of sweat. Her full breasts were pointed toward the sky as she continued to stretch. Seka rolled onto her hands and knees, stretching her back again, this time pushing her pert apple bottom into the air. A cool breeze blew in from the sea, caressing her bare ass and its soft embrace, prying a gasp from her lips in the process. Satisfied, Seka released her breath and lay her head down on her arms, closing her eyes again.

She hadn't realized how much she'd missed the beach the last few years of her life. It didn't matter to the ebony vixen as she lay nude on her towel, utterly alone. She brought a bottle of champagne with her, but that was empty now, letting her head float with the lazy clouds overhead. The clouds seemed to be the most important thing in the world right then. Where had they come from? More importantly, where were they headed in such a rush? Surely the clouds wanted to stare at her some more.

Smiling at the incredibly vain thought, Seka looked at her wicker picnic basket reaching in for a piece of cheese to nibble on. She didn't feel vain even though she was sexy, incredibly sexy. She knew because when she dropped her daughter off at school, the husbands stared, and the mothers glared angrily. She knew because when she signed up for college, she was offered two modeling jobs and a career in the adult industry. She might have accepted one of the offers if she was not married. Instead, she'd stuck with her office job for a large company. Still, she knew that men wanted her, and most wanted her because of her ass.

"Fuck." Seka muttered as her pussy started to moisten again. The more she thought about men staring at her, wanting her, the wetter she got. Men with their hard chests, hard cocks, hard grips, the idea of them was enough to get her clit to throb, and her thighs quivered, summoning her hand between them.

Seka caught her clit between two fingers, gently scissoring the tiny nub of flesh as thoughts of men cavorted behind her closed eyelids. All sizes and colors, one after the other. Slender cute track boys with toned thighs and tight butts that would go all night; buff chiseled men who could lift her with one arm and fuck her standing; long-haired rock and roll guys with full sleeve tattoos who would push her to do things she could never repeat; and chubby computer nerds who would cum the moment she smiled in their direction.

Two fingers slipped into her slicked hole and slowly twisted deeper into her body. At first, she bit down on her lip, stifling the scream building up in her chest, but then she remembered; she was alone, and no one would hear her scream. Her lips parted, and she squealed. The squeals turned to moans a few seconds later, timed with the pair of fingers plunging in and out of her sex. The heel of her hand was pressed against her clit, grinding against her hip bone, sending jolts of pleasure along her spine and finally to her nipples.

"Mmmm!" Seka gasped, her legs tangling in the towel as she rolled over onto her back. One foot digging into the warm sand, the other wrapped in the fabric as she spread her legs indecently wide and continued to pleasure herself. Her free hands gravitated towards her aching nipples, pinching down on one then and gently twisting. "God yes!" Her chest was heaving with each ragged breath she pulled into her chest.

Her mouth opened wide as she twisted her fingers inside her hitting the sweet spot that set off explosions in her head. Her thighs cinched together, trapping her hand between them as her muscles clenched down in quick spasms. They continued to send tiny quakes through her body for several minutes, finally subsiding and letting Seka relax onto the towel, softly mewling as the afterglow of her orgasm spread over her.

The clouds had gone entirely while she played with herself, leaving a pure blue sky with a deep orange sun that would soon journey beyond the horizon to kids in Hawaii, Japan, or someplace on the other side of the world where it was still nighttime, and people were sleeping.

She placed both hands on her buttocks and started to rub slowly. The coolness of her hands perfectly countered the heat in her cheeks. While unplanned, the sensations these simple actions brought were sending fresh signals to her damp pussy, little thrills of pleasure that did not want to go away.

She knew she'd originally planned to have some fun this evening, but could she really last another 2 hours feeling this horny?

4 minutes. That was the quickest she'd ever been able to achieve orgasm. Granted, she had been really horny for days, so she didn't think it could happen again, but she had to do something. She didn't fancy the thought of sitting at her desk all afternoon, her thoughts running wild.

Even before she'd sat down completely, she glanced down and saw how wet the crouch on her pants was. "Oh," she groaned in embarrassment. Was that really from the spanking earlier? She slipped her left hand in between her thighs, bringing her middle finger up towards her pussy. Her finger slipped easily into the hot juices. She must be soaking she thought, as she dragged her finger slowly in between her engorged lips, stroking it up to her hardened erect clit, which she suspected had snuck out from under its hood before she'd even sat down.

Even the most delicate of touches sent electrical shocks through her crotch. She raised her hand out from between her legs to check. The tip of her finger was covered in traces of fluid; she raised it slowly to her face and inhaled.

She'd never been too hung up on tasting herself, but she adored the smell. It was so basic, an exquisite musky scent intended solely to arouse, just as it was doing now. While she slipped her right hand in between her legs to follow the same tracks covered by the left, she closed her eyes, opened her mouth slowly, and tentatively stuck out her hot pink tongue. Grazing the tip of the juice covering her fingers before pressing it into her mouth and sucking off her taste.

She moaned, before slowly rubbing her clit with her right hand, index, and middle finger, slowly rotating over her engorged clit. Every slight graze increases the wetness between her legs. She started to squeeze the nipple of her left breast through the fabric. It was already erect, but the gentle pressure caused the sensitive flesh to tighten even more, forcing a gentle moan from her lips. At the same time, she was slowly increasing the speed of her fingers on her clit. The gentle electric sensations from before were building into the occasional shockwave, causing her whole body to twitch slightly. Her left hand slid under her

24

left thigh to try and reach her sopping wet pussy; if she contorted her hand around far enough, she could just get her middle finger to glide into the tight wet entrance to her pussy. She let out an involuntary little yelp! She started to slide her finger slowly in and out, pressing harder on her clit with the right hand, delighting at the little shocks it was sending through her body.

Each gentle pulse increased the wetness. She was so aroused now that she barely paused before withdrawing her middle finger and bringing it slowly to her mouth, poking her tongue out again to lap at her warm fragrant juices.

The speed of her rubbing increased, her right leg starting to twitch each time she caught her clit just right, the shockwave pulses increasing in both frequency and strength. She bit her lower lip stifling another cry, just a few more…

The day would have been perfect if the blaring sound of her cell phone had not disturbed her pleasant haze a few moments too soon and back into reality. "Yeah, baby. I'll be home in a bit." She said, smiling at her phone. It was her husband, and the thought of him waiting for her made her still-slick fingers migrate southward. It would be at least another half hour before she managed to get home, excited about the night and its memories.

SPILLED JUICE

As Clarice dressed according to her husband's specifications, she wondered what her sex life would be like if she had been given a different name at birth. Her husband, Andrew, felt that because Clarice had been given the name of a relative that lived 100 years ago, she should dress the part. Clarice, a housewife, was required to wear old-fashioned dresses, stockings, heels, and of course pearls. Regardless of her schedule, you would always see Clarice dressed according to her husband's demands. Today was no different. Or was it?

After Clarice started preparing dinner for her family, her husband, and two children, 19 and 14 years old, she sat down for some serious, quiet time. She did not know why, but today she really needed to clear her head, so she decided to have a glass of wine and a few of her favorite chocolates. As she finished her wine, there was a knock at the door. Thinking it was a neighbor, she invited the guest in. When she looked up, much to her surprise, it was not the neighbor at all but her oldest son's best friend, Patrick. He and her son were the same age; however, Patrick appeared more mature, better developed physically, and incredibly sexy. She invited him to have a seat and offered him a glass of juice. He was too young for alcohol, and she was not about to have him start drinking now. He accepted her offer. They sat and chatted for a while.

Surprisingly, Patrick found himself aroused by this innocent exchange of small talk and laughter. Clarice was also startled by this sudden burst of sexual chemistry. Twenty-five years his senior, she tried to convince herself that this was her imagination. There was no way she could be attracted to someone the same age as her son, but his every move exuded sex. And the longer he sat, the harder he became to resist. In this awkward moment, Clarice accidentally knocked Patrick's glass on the floor. They both reached for the glass at the same time. As Patrick touched Clarice's hand, the sexual desire was impossible to deny. Clarice quickly removed her hand and rushed to the refrigerator to refill the glass. Patrick followed. What happened next would be a night to remember for the rest of Clarice's life.

With tenderness, Patrick turned Clarice around to face him. He gently leaned her against the refrigerator and began to caress her chest, carefully outlining the neck of the dress. Taking his cues from Clarice's breathing pattern, he then opens a few buttons, just enough to expose her bra. With his fingertips, he made circles around her nipples, and as her nipples hardened, he pinched them with his mouth, careful not to disturb her bra. Clarice attempted to resist, but the more Patrick pinched her nipples with his lips, the wetter her pussy got. Never in her life had she felt her pussy and her body so aroused.

Just as she thought this could not get any better, Patrick finished unbuttoning her dress, exposing her bra, stockings, and panties. He became extremely turned on by the sight of Clarice's wet, glistening pussy. With his tongue, he kissed and nibbled her body, starting with her nipples and ending up with her pussy. He parted her voluptuous pussy lips with his tongue and found her clit anxiously awaiting his discovery. She grabbed his head, guiding him to her favorite spot while praying that he would never stop.

Patrick's cock, 12 inches in length and 4 inches wide, throbbed, reminding Patrick that it, too, needed attention. Patrick guided Clarice to the floor, placed her on her back, and gently parted her legs. Clarice and her husband always made love in the bedroom. Patrick had the biggest cock she had ever seen. His cock and the lure of having sex someplace other than the bedroom made her eager to please him. Patrick took his cock and spanked the wet juicy pussy in front of him, teasing it, making it hotter, and causing it to squirt more juices. He put his face in her pussy and used his tongue to bring her to the brink of an orgasm. Just before Clarice was about to cum, Patrick stopped, denying her the ultimate release.

This made Clarice hotter and more determined to serve him as much pussy as he wanted. He took his cock and put it in the entrance of her pussy. Clarice resisted. Patrick whispered in her ear, "just the head I'll only put the head in." Reluctantly she agreed. As he gently put the head in, Clarice felt an insatiable tingle throughout her body and began to beg for more. Patrick wanted to satisfy his cock by feeling every inch of this wet delectable pussy. He gently glided deeper and savored every minute. The deeper he went, the harder his cock got. Finally, Clarice's pussy had taken all 12 inches of his cock. This was a first for Patrick. Girls, his age could not handle his size. He could not find words to describe what he was feeling. With each stroke, both Patrick and Clarice wanted more.

As Clarice was about to reach her orgasm, Patrick again pulled out. Before Clarice could voice her frustration, Patrick shoved his cock in her mouth. He repeatedly forced his cock down her throat. After she sucked all her pussy juices from his cock, Patrick reentered her pussy. His cock craved this dark, wet, juicy place and he was ecstatic to accommodate this desire. Again, his dick was saturated with Clarice's pussy. His throbbing member desired more. He nibbled her neck and like a gentleman asked if he could put the head of his cock in her ass. Filled with an incredible thirst, Clarice consented. Patrick first teased her ass with his finger first and next used his tongue to bring intense pleasure to her ass.

He was ravenous, now burying his head deep between her tits, kissing, caressing, nibbling at her soft nipples. He had lost all sense of self-control, and now all he wanted to do was devour her.

She, in turn, reacted powerfully, moaning, and gasping at each touch, tease, kiss, lick, and bite. She held his head to her as he first sucked on one nipple, then the other. He was like a starving man seeing food for the first time.

By now, he was rock hard and could feel his prick pushing against her, desperate to discard boxers and panties and slip into her welcoming warmth.

As he continued to suck on her nipple, she bent her head down to his ear and whispered,

"Do you want to fuck me again?"

He stopped, removed his head from her breasts, and looked up at her smiling face. He didn't need to reply. She pushed him onto the floor and kissed him as her hand moved down, slipping into his boxers. She was not as young as Patrick, but she knew how to handle a cock, slowly teasing it with her hand, and her supple body writhed over him.

He slid his hands down and grabbed her plump yet firm ass, sliding one hand down over the fabric of her panties and entering at the side. She gasped as his fingers slid across her slick slit, and he was amazed at how wet she was. He gently rubbed her opening, wondering whether he should explore with his fingers first or save it for his cock. He decided on the latter and slid his hand further into her panties, across her swollen lips, and up to her clit.

"Oh, fucking yes," she moaned as the tip of his index finger glided smoothly over her little mound, her hips grinding against his hand. As he rubbed, her grip on his dick got tighter and tighter, and he was worried for a moment that she might rip it off.

But just as quickly, she let go, removing her hand from his boxers. She sat and fell to her knees, pulling his boxers down in one smooth action. His heavy prick shot up straight, and without a second thought, she took it all in her mouth.

Jesus Christ, he thought as this "magic lady" deep-throated him with no warm-up. She's got no fucking gag reflex.

He felt her take him deeper and deeper into her mouth, the tip of his dick touching the back of her throat, and her not so much as flinch.

There was no hesitation in her actions, eager yet practiced. And as she continued to suck him off, she slipped her hand under and started working his balls, caressing them in her palm.

He laid back and gave into the sensation, enjoying the moment. During this encounter, she had told him so many fantastical stories about her sucking dick like a champion prior to her getting married, and now he knew they were all true, and what's more, he was now one of them! Her husband had no idea what he was missing.

He moaned and bucked his hips as she ran her tongue gently around the head of his cock, teasing him, tasting his pre-cum, before taking it all again into her warm, wet mouth.

He moaned, and she took his dick out of her mouth, working the shaft, wet with saliva, with her hand.

"You can cum in my mouth if you want," she said. "As long as you've got more for after."

Then, without waiting for a reply, she began sucking his dick faster and faster, and the more he moaned, the faster she worked it.

"I'm Cumming," he said, as he felt the tension build in his balls. "I'm cumming."

And with that, he bucked up his hips and filled her welcoming mouth with strand after strand of his jizz. Still, it did not faze her, her head still sucking on that dick even after she had milked it for all it was worth.

Finally, she slid the dick out of her mouth, her soft lips caressing the shaft one final time as she did so. A thin trail of spittle and jizz ran from her lips to the tip of his dick, and she scooped it up with her finger and put it in her mouth.

He laid back exhausted, and she climbed on top of him, looking down, smiling. He smiled back, and she opened her mouth, showing him the big load he had shot in there. She dribbled it down three inches, then sucked it back in, swallowing it all. She opened her mouth again, and it was empty. She leaned in to kiss him, and he could taste himself on her lips.

He was still hard, and she was rubbing her panty-covered pussy on his dick. If he'd had it in him, he would have flipped her over and fucked her brains out. But he knew he had to wait a minute. Still, they were in a state of disequilibrium, and he knew that wasn't fair.

"You like that?" She asked. "Did you like when I swallowed your cum?"

"I really fucking did," he said, breathlessly "but not as much as I'm going to enjoy this." With that, he flipped her onto her back, pinning her down, kissing her mouth, moving down her body, letting her arms go as he kissed down her breasts, over her flat belly, then down over her panties. She moaned as he lay gentle kisses across the fabric, soaked with her juices.

He kissed her inner thighs, and she squirmed as he ran a single finger up and down her panties.

"Don't tease me," she said. "I can't stand it."

He knew it was true; he could see her wetness, smell her desire. There was only one thing she wanted right now, and he was going to give it to her.

He gently took hold of her panties by her hips and slowly dragged them down. She wriggled to give him space to operate, and he gently peeled them off her swollen lips, to which they were stuck with her juices.

He slipped them off one leg, then the other. He admired their wetness and smiled at the face. She had gotten so wet for him, for his dick, and she had not had it in her yet, not properly, at least.

He kneeled in front of her spread legs and admired her perfect pussy, trimmed and shaved, perfect for eating. He moved in closer, inhaling her scent deeply. He wanted to remember this moment forever. He held his breath, closed his eyes, and sat there in quiet contemplation, his hands running gently up and down the outside of her thighs.

"Are you ok?" She asked.

"Perfect," he said, running his tongue up her damp pussy.

"Oh fuck," she moaned as he got to work. With his balls empty, he was driven not by passion but by the pure desire to eat her pussy, to lick and tease her until she achieved the perfect orgasm.

Clarice had never experienced anything like this, and at that moment, she gave her body totally to Patrick. Being aware of the size of his cock, Patrick gently and very slowly entered her ass until his entire cock was submerged in this hot juicy place. With even rhythmic motions, he slowly fucked her ass.

Clarice would moan with pain, but Patrick reassured her that she was satisfying him. Clarice enjoyed this mixture of pain and pleasure, allowing Patrick to find satisfaction in this forbidden act. But Patrick still craved more.

He pulled out, turned Clarice over, put her on her hands and knees, took his belt and placed it tightly around her neck, and put his cock back in her ass. As he fucked her ass, his right hand was caressing her clit, and within minutes Clarice came. Her body shook as she came, and Patrick did not let up. Clarice came again, again, and again. Now it was Patrick's turn. He pulled out of her ass and put his thick sticky juice on her ass between her cheeks. They both collapsed and wondered how this happened over a glass of spilled juice. What a night to remember.

SOME THINGS YOU CAN'T DO ALONE

After weeks of working long days, odd numbers of hours, and weekends, Adriana finally had a break. Craving excitement and desperate to experience something new, Adriana decided to hit the town to find a hot low-key club for a drink, dancing, and just maybe a little flirting. She slipped into a little black dress choosing the sexiest underwear she could find. If a little something happened, she wanted them to enjoy every inch of the experience. 5-inch stilettos completed her outfit for the night.

After driving around for about half-hour, she spotted just the place. She parked the car, made her way into the club, took a seat near the back, and ordered her favorite drink. She likes her drinks like she likes her men, strong and uncomplicated.

As she sipped her drink, a handsome, extremely handsome younger man with a "down for whatever look" sent her a drink. As she accepted the drink, she winked at him and blew a kiss at the generous gesture. She asked the waiter to extend an invitation to Mr. "Down for whatever Handsome" to join her. He quickly accepted, and soon she was face to face with her next adventure.

After they finished their drinks, they decided to leave. Adriana invited him to take a ride with her to explore some of her favorite spots. Little did he know how much fun they would have in her favorite place, which also included private cabanas.

She had been wanting to seduce him and now was her chance.

They parked in an open secluded area, and she whispered into his ear. They got out of the car, and he anxiously followed her lead. They took off their clothes, and it was not long before they were making out in a secluded spot. Enjoying the skillful cock of this younger man, she pushed him away so she could put his cock in her mouth. Satisfying her men orally has always been a big turn-on for Adriana.

His cock was so big that she could feel his cock at the back of her throat, causing her to gag. She sucked his cock until it could not swell anymore.

Now his turn. He licked her gently, his senses attuned to the slightest movements and changes in behavior. This was all about her, about her pleasure, and he was damn sure he was going to give her the time of her life. As far as he was concerned, she was generous enough to share her delicious pussy with him, so he should show her the utmost respect by eating the fuck out of it.

He licked, and she moaned, and he knew she was close because he knew how much sucking dick turned her on. She had told him many times tonight, and now he was taking advantage of it. He circled her clit and sliding his hand onto her well-trimmed pubic hair, raised it slightly, lifting the clitoral hood and exposing her pleasure center to his mouth. He formed a protective seal over it with his mouth and began to suck gently.

"Oh, my fucking god," she moaned, "what the fuck are you doing?"

He wanted to stop and ask if she liked it, but as she pushed her pussy deeper into his face, he got his answer.

He let go of one of her thighs, both of which were now securely clamped to the sides of his head and began to run it up and down her slit, feeling her wetness.

He had thought of saving it for later, but he knew now that this was the best way to show her an exciting time. He lowered his index finger and slowly slipped it into her warm cunt. She gasped at the sensation and moaned deeply as he began to gently stroke the underside of her clit, stimulating her g-spot.

As he continued, she began to writhe uncontrollably, and he knew she was on the cusp. He kept going, knowing there was one surefire way to send her over the edge. So, not changing anything, he slipped his other hand from her thigh and ran it underneath her, caressing her ass as he went.

"Oh fuck," she said, and he sensed she knew what was going to happen next.

His hand continued to slide over her and downwards until one finger slid across her ass, slipping between the cheeks until it found her asshole.

"Oh fuck," she moaned as the tip of his index finger gently caressed her quivering hole. She bucked and writhed and pushed her ass down on his finger, the tip gently slipping into her.

She lifted and dropped her ass, trying to fuck his finger as his other finger occupied her pussy and his mouth sucked on her clit.

"Oh, my fucking fuck," she moaned, her hips grinding faster and faster, harder and harder, as he kept the same rhythm, the same tempo, letting her find the precise combination that would get her off. He continued and felt her pussy juices flowing down his hand as he continued to finger her pussy.

She rode faster and faster, and she moaned loudly, throwing her head one way then the other, bucking against his hand. She reached down and grabbed his hair, pulling at it, pulling him in closer.

It hurt, but still, he didn't stop. He had waited a long time to eat that pussy, and he was going to make damn sure she fucking remembered it.

Finally, he felt her hand gripping his hair slacken and release, and he slowed to a halt, gently removing his lips from her clit, sliding out his soaking wet finger from her pussy, and, finally, sliding the tip of his index finger out of her quivering asshole.

He stood and looked at her prone body. She was exhausted, her red hair stuck to her pale face, dripping with sweat. She looked him in the eye and smiled, and he knew this would be an orgasm she would never forget.

Still, he thought, they weren't done yet, as he lay next to her.

"Enjoy that?" he asked.

Unable to speak, she nodded her head slightly in the affirmative.

"Well, here's dessert," he said, slipping his finger covered in her wetness into her mouth. She sucked on it, savoring her taste, and then he pulled it out of her mouth and kissed her deeply, his mouth covered in her juices as well.

She rubbed her wet fingertips across his lips, and his tongue shot out, devouring every drop of her passion. Once again, he was overcome with lust, with an insatiable urge to have that red-haired pussy.

He rolled her onto her back and with one smooth motion, slid himself inside her. She moaned as his hard cock entered her warmness, her wetness allowing him easy access before her pussy walls tensed on his shaft.

He began to move slowly, savoring every moment, every unique move and feel of her. He had imagined how good this would feel a million times, but he never expected anything like this. It was as if her pussy was made especially for his dick.

"Oh, yes," she moaned, evidently feeling the same way. "Give it all to me."

He worked, pushing his dick in a little deeper each time until he was fully balls-deep in her eager cunt. He began to move faster and faster, and she moaned louder and louder. Soon, he was looking down on her, fucking her as hard as he could.

Damn, he could fuck her like this forever, but he knew this might be the only chance he got, so he didn't want to waste it. Without warning, he pulled himself out of her pussy.

"What are you doing?" She asked, mystified.

She let out a little yelp as he grabbed her by her hips and pulled her ass close to him and led her to the Cabana.

"I want to see those beautiful tits," he said, sliding himself back into her. Within seconds he was pounding her silly again, him standing, his hands on her hips. As he threw his dick into her, he watched her writhe and moan in the Cabana, helpless with pleasure, her giant tits swaying with the motion of her body.

He continued to fuck her before sucking on his thumb and beginning to gently massage her clit as he fucked her.

It was putting off his rhythm slightly, but he wanted to make sure she was enjoying it as much as possible. But then her hand came down and batted his thumbs away. She slid her fingers down her lips and brought them back up to her clit, rubbing it for all she was worth.

He returned his hand to her hips and got back into the steady rhythm. He gazed down, watching this beautiful woman finger herself as he pounded the ever-loving shit out of her ruby-red pussy.

He felt he was once again getting close, and though he could have happily cum inside her exactly like this, the image of her big tits bouncing as she fingered herself, there was still one more thing he wanted to try.

"Do you want me to fuck you from behind?" He asked, not stopping.

"Oh. Fuck. Yes. Please." She panted, gasping for breath as she continued to take his dick.

He knew this would be her answer. She told him this was one of her favorite positions, and he was desperate to see why she liked it so much.

He pulled his dick out of her drenched pussy, and she took a moment to catch her breath before getting on her hand and knees on the edge of the Cabana.

Then she placed his swollen cock in her pussy and stroked him until he started to cum. She pulled him out of her pussy and encouraged him to put his hot semen on her face. As he continued to jerk off using her mouth and face, Ariana became even hotter, and he was ready for more. Now on her hands and knees, she gently guided him into her

39

ass; anal was her favorite. Hypnotized by the tightness of her ass, he unloaded his full load in her ass.

Exhausted and satisfied, he begins to redress, wondering if he could see her again.

This is a night he would remember.

www.ingramcontent.com/pod-product-compliance
Lightning Source LLC
Chambersburg PA
CBHW071318200626
46813CB00015B/2257